WELCOME TO

Beast Quest

Collect the special coins in this book.
You will earn one gold coin for
every chapter you read.

Once you have finished all the chapters,
find out what to do with your gold coins at
the back of the book.

With special thanks to Elizabeth Galloway

For Jake Lovegrove. Wishing you many adventures!

www.beastquest.co.uk

ORCHARD BOOKS

First published in Great Britain in 2011 by The Watts Publishing Group
This edition published in 2016 by The Watts Publishing Group

5 7 9 10 8 6 4

Text © 2011 Beast Quest Limited.
Cover and inside illustrations by Steve Sims © Beast Quest Limited 2011

Beast Quest is a registered trademark of Beast Quest Limited
Series created by Beast Quest Limited, London

A CIP catalogue record for this book is available from the British Library.

ISBN 978 1 40831 312 1

Printed in Great Britain

The paper and board used in this book are made from wood from responsible sources

Orchard Books
An imprint of Hachette Children's Group
Part of The Watts Publishing Group Limited
Carmelite House, 50 Victoria Embankment, London EC4Y 0DZ

An Hachette UK Company
www.hachette.co.uk
www.hachettechildrens.co.uk

Beast Quest®

HECTON
THE BODY
SNATCHER

BY ADAM BLADE

ORCHARD

THE

WESTERN OCEAN

THE FOREST OF FEAR

THE V

THE RUBY DESERT

SPI

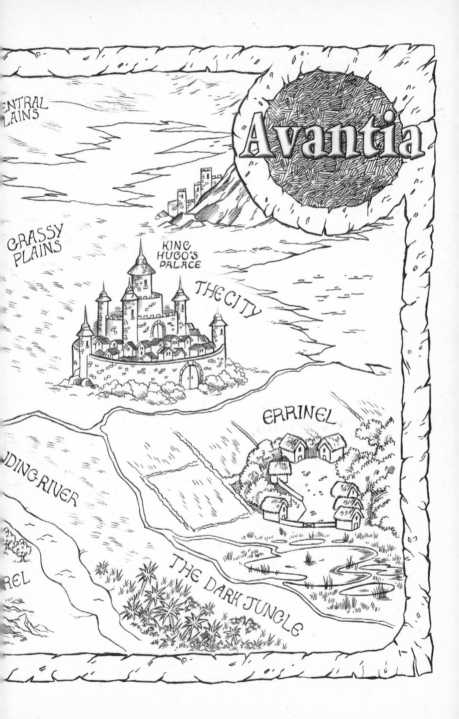

CONTENTS

Tremble, warriors of Avantia, for a new enemy stalks your land!

I am Sanpao, the Pirate King of Makai! My ship brings me to your shores to claim an ancient magic more powerful than any you've encountered before. No one can stand in my way, especially not that pathetic boy, Tom, or his friends. Even Aduro cannot help you this time. My pirate crew will pillage and burn without mercy, and my Beasts will be more than a match for any hero in Avantia.

Pirates! Batten down the hatches and raise the sails. We come to conquer and destroy!

Sanpao the Pirate King

PROLOGUE

Sandric the Tree Dweller grabbed the vine rope that hung outside his family's hut, and swung through the Vanished Woodland. He gave a shout of exhilaration as he let go of the vine, caught hold of another, and whipped past a group of startled women sewing bark tunics. The Woodland was hidden in a secret valley of Avantia, a fold in the earth tucked into the foot of the volcano. Few visitors ever came across the Tree Dwellers. Their huts, bridges and vines, all suspended high in the canopy, had remained undisturbed for generations. Sandric had never seen anyone from outside his own tribe. He swung through the Vanished Woodland. The vine rope swept upwards in a steep arc and he let go, flinging his arms above his head. He soared like a bird above the tops of the trees, the grey slopes of the volcano looming ahead, then dropped down into the green canopy.

Branches snapped and splintered as Sandric swung among the tree tops. When he reached the glade at the centre of the Vanished

Woodland, he seized a ladder woven from creepers. He scrambled up it, crawled onto a thick branch, and gasped. There it was – a tree unlike any he'd seen before.

It was enormous, its twisting branches stretching high above the canopy. The leaves were fresh and a waxy green. He gazed down the broad column of the trunk, and saw that the soil around its base was loose. The tree must have thrust, fully formed, from the ground.

But why has it come here? he wondered. A large, grey flake drifted onto the back of his hand. He sniffed it. It smelt of flame and smoke.

"The Fire Mountain is awake," he muttered.

He raised himself up on his branch and peered over the treetops. In the distance a dark cloud hung on the horizon, over the volcano. Orange flames sparked from the crater and the cloud billowed and grew, moving towards the Vanished Woodland. More flakes of ash fluttered around him, catching on his clothes and clinging to the leaves and branches.

Sandric slid down the ladder and grabbed the vine. He swooped back to the huts, yelling, "Orange Heat! The Fire Mountain is angry!"

The other Tree Dwellers scattered, running and leaping from branch to branch to shelter inside their huts. Tendrils of smoke coiled around the trees. Sandric coughed as the acrid fumes filled his lungs. He lost his grip and slithered down the vine, almost to the ground.

A huge figure stepped out from the smoke. He had the body of a man, thickset and muscular, but with green flesh. His cloak seemed to be made from feathers and fur.

It billowed out as the figure drew nearer, and Sandric saw a fox's brush on one shoulder, a crushed rabbit on the other. A hollowed-out bull's head formed the cloak's hood, with gleaming curled horns.

It's all made from dead creatures, Sandric realised. Sweat trickled down his back.

The Beast gave a roar so loud that it seemed to shudder through Sandric. He pulled the cloak more tightly around him, and to Sandric's horror the half-rotten bodies of the cloak groaned, their eyes rolling back in their heads as their gruesome stitching stretched.

Sandric was shaking so violently he could barely grip the vine. He scrambled up it, his hands and feet slipping and sliding.

When he glanced down, however, the Beast's yellow eyes were fixed on him, the green skin of his face contorted into a smile. In one hand he held a trident, its three points glittering through the smoke, and in the other a net fringed with sharp metal barbs.

The Beast gave a furious hiss and something snared around Sandric, tangling his limbs so he couldn't climb. It was the net. He fell in a crumpled heap on the woodland floor.

"No one can help you now," the Beast mocked him, his voice deeper than the groan of a collapsing tree. "Hecton is here."

The Beast strode towards him. Sandric tried to scramble away, but with a snarl Hecton raised his trident and hurled it at him. The three blades pierced his hand, pinning Sandric to the ground. He cried out as his flesh sang with pain.

Hecton gripped the edges of his cloak, spreading it wide, and leapt up. As the Beast flew through the air, Sandric saw more dead bodies suspended from the lining of his cloak – stoats, weasels, toads, their eyes blinking – and realised what this Beast was.

A body snatcher...

The ground shuddered as Hecton landed in a crouch over Sandric. He straddled Sandric's torso, his fists pressed into the ground either side of Sandric's head. Hecton grinned, and a trickle of yellow drool splattered onto Sandric's forehead. The Beast opened his mouth wide and a green mist wafted out, coiling around Sandric's arms and legs. The bull's head hood of his cloak fell back, revealing a writhing mass of worms instead of hair.

"Spare me—" Sandric started to scream. But as the mist wound down his throat, tiredness swept over him, making his eyelids droop. He stopped struggling. With a sucking noise, his body lifted into the cloak, his limbs fitting among the rotten flesh of the other creatures.

Hecton, Sandric thought. *Master.*

FLIGHT IN THE FOG

Tom narrowed his eyes against the grey fog. Through the mist, he could see Tagus the Horse-Man cantering away across Avantia's Grassy Plains.

"Farewell!" Tom called to him. "And thank you."

Tagus had helped Tom and Elenna defeat Koron – an Evil Beast in the thrall of Sanpao the Pirate King. Tom shuddered as he remembered Koron's deadly claws and stinging tail; Tagus had helped them defeat him.

The fog rolled in waves, weaving around thickly and making Storm and Blizzard, their two horses, whinny uneasily.

Elenna licked her finger and held it in the air. "Look," she said, showing her hand to Tom. It was covered in a thin coating of grit. "This isn't ordinary fog."

A distant rumble shuddered through the ground and to the east a column of orange light shot up, dazzling against the dim sky. There was an explosive roar, and a shower of grey flakes fell around them, clinging to their tunics and dusting the horses' coats. Tom coughed, wiping the dust from his eyes.

"The volcano at Stonewin is erupting," he said. "This isn't fog – it's volcanic ash."

There was another rumble, like a clap of thunder deep within the earth. Storm reared up on his hind legs, neighing with alarm.

"Easy, boy," Tom soothed his faithful stallion. To Elenna, he said, "If only I had my jewelled belt, I could ask Epos to let us know what's happening. I hope she's all right," he added. The volcano was the flame bird's home.

Tom had won his magical belt many Quests ago. It was studded with jewels that afforded him special powers; the red jewel gave him the ability to understand the Beasts. But Sanpao had placed Aduro, the Good Wizard of Avantia, under an evil enchantment and Aduro had magicked the jewelled belt around Sanpao's waist, giving the pirate king its powers. In its place, the wizard had given Tom a length of hide knotted across his waist. Tom had slotted the fang left by Koron inside it; after he defeated each of Sanpao's Beasts, it left behind a token. Each token had a mysterious power, but could only be used once.

Elenna opened Storm's saddlebag and pulled out a rolled-up map. It was made from the bark of the Tree of Being. The Tree was a magical gateway to all realms, and Sanpao and his pirate crew were determined to capture it: possession of the Tree would allow them to loot and pillage wherever they pleased. It was Tom's Quest to stop this happening, but he and Elenna had other reasons to defeat the pirates, too. Tom's mother, Freya, and Elenna's beloved pet wolf, Silver, were trapped in the strange land of Tavania; the Tree of Being could create a portal to this other kingdom, and was their only hope of rescuing them.

Tom unfurled the map. The outline of the kingdom was etched into the bark. Tom scanned the familiar landscape, where he and Elenna had shared so many adventures.

"Elenna, look at this." He jabbed a finger at the picture of a wooded valley, tucked beside the volcano.

He read the lettering printed below the image.

THE VANISHED WOODLAND.

"I've never heard of it before," said Elenna. "We've travelled all over

Avantia, but there are still places we haven't seen."

The tiny outline of the Tree of Being appeared at the centre of the woodland picture. The Tree didn't grow in one fixed place, but moved around so it would be safe from attack. It sprang from the ground, fully formed, before disappearing into the earth once more. Tom and Elenna had to travel quickly to each new location to reach it before the pirates.

"So that's where we need to go," said Tom.

"And where we'll meet the next Beast," Elenna added.

Tom nodded. Sanpao had warned that the next Beast they faced would be the most terrible yet.

Tom returned the map to Storm's saddlebag.

The stallion tossed his head, flicking away ash. Tom patted Storm's neck, while Elenna combed her fingers through Blizzard's mane. The snow-white mare had been given to her by Abraham the Horse Whisperer, who they'd rescued from Sanpao's thrall. Blizzard shied away from the tumbling ash, whinnying fearfully. Elenna leaned low over her, stroking her mane again as she murmured reassuring words.

"She's getting used to you." Tom grinned as Blizzard calmed down. "Silver will be jealous."

Elenna looked down at the ground. Tom felt a tug of guilt.

"You'll see him again," he promised. "We'll defeat Sanpao and get Silver and my mother back."

They nudged their horses into a canter, across the Grassy Plains. The nearer they got to the volcano, the thicker the ash hung in the air. It was becoming warmer, too; Tom could feel the dust sticking to his damp skin. Elenna's face was streaked with grime, like she'd fallen into a pile of cinders. A puff of flakes swirled around them, and Tom spluttered as they filled his lungs.

"Pull your collar up," called Elenna, yanking her own over her nose and mouth. Tom did the same, and found he could breathe more easily. Stopping briefly, they took out

the blankets they slept in at night
from Storm's saddlebag. They draped
them over the noses of their horses
and secured them to the bridles.

They galloped through the rippling
expanse of grass, soaring over
ditches and wading through streams.
They had been travelling for almost
a full day when the ground became
firmer, and the horses' hooves
clattered over rocks and pebbles.
Looming through the ash was a
distant village.

"I know this place," Tom called
across to Elenna.

He raised a hand above his eyes,
squinting into the distance. He could
make out half-collapsed buildings.
Plumes of smoke billowed from them,

mingling with the ash in the sky.

"What happened here?" Elenna wondered aloud.

They drew closer and saw a column of people pouring out of the village. Men and women were carrying bundles on their backs. They could hear the sobs and cries of children as

their parents hurried them along.

A shout rose up from among the villagers: "Look – they've come to help us! Over here! Please help."

The people rushed towards them through the ash and thronged about Storm and Blizzard, their faces pale and their eyes wide with terror.

A bearded man stepped up to Tom. "Our village has been ransacked by a – Oh, it's terrible!" The man broke down, sobbing.

Tom felt sure he knew who had harmed these people. There was only one group of men capable of such evil in Avantia.

"Pirates," Tom muttered, angrily. "Elenna, this is all down to Sanpao's ferocious men!"

1

THE RAIDED VILLAGE

"We were sheltering indoors from the ash cloud," said a woman with a baby on her hip. "They've helped themselves to our food – and they tore apart our houses." The mother glanced at the child she was holding, her face crumpling. "They snatched my boy," she said. "I couldn't hold on to him!"

"A recruit, they said!" hissed the bearded man. "A pirate recruit!"

Tom looked at Elenna. They both knew what it was to be torn from their families. *I won't let this happen to these children,* Tom thought.

Tom drew his sword. "Head for the City," he told the villagers. "That should be far enough away from the pirates. While there's blood in my veins, we won't rest until we've defeated them."

As the villagers did as Tom asked, the woman with the baby looked up at Tom. Tears were running down her face. "Those pirates have my Aaron," she said. "Please find him!"

Tom thought of his mother and Silver, so far from home. "We'll get him back," he said. "I swear it."

Storm and Blizzard cantered towards the ruined village. Tom glanced back and saw the woman watching them go, her baby clasped to her. He drew his collar up, squinting against the swirling flakes of ash. The sun was starting to set, tingeing the grey sky with orange.

As they approached the village, Tom saw that most of it had been reduced to piles of rubble. A flag had been hoisted up one of the remaining towers, emblazoned with the outline of a Beast's skull. *Sanpao's symbol,* Tom thought.

Elenna was pointing at the defensive wall that circled the village. "Look," she said.

It was lined with Sanpao's pirates. Weapons gleamed cruelly in their hands – Tom could see crossbows and cat-o'-nine-tails; even heavy iron balls swung on chains. The skull symbol was tattooed on the pirates' chests in ebony ink.

"Hold it straight, brat," one of the pirates bawled. Tom saw a young boy standing among them, struggling to hold a cutlass. It was almost as large as he was. "Want your mummy to help?" the pirate sneered. "Well, guess what? She's not here!" The pirates cackled with laughter.

"That must be Aaron," Elenna said. Her eyes flashed angrily as she looked around. "Where's Sanpao?"

"I can't see him anywhere," Tom

replied, scanning the row of men
for the pirate king. "Maybe he's left
them here to loot while he goes after
the Tree."

Tom knew he had to get the new
recruit away – and then track down

Sanpao and the Tree of Life. He and Elenna halted in front of the village gate. The pirates leered down at them, laughing and brandishing their weapons.

"Look who it is! Not learnt your lesson yet, you scrawny scallywags?" the pirate who had been mocking Aaron yelled. A gold tooth at the front of his mouth glittered.

Another man, with a long scar around his neck, flicked his cat-o'-nine-tails towards Tom and Elenna. "I reckon they be wanting a taste of my cat."

As the pirates laughed darkly, Tom raised his sword. "Cowards! You can't loot defenceless villagers and steal their children!"

"Oh, can't we?" said the pirate with the gold tooth. He held his arms wide, gesturing to the other men. "You may not have noticed, you mangy dogs, but we're pirates! Stealing and looting is what we do." He grabbed Aaron's shoulder. "This brat here's just the start," he said. "We'll soon have a new crew of boys trained and ready."

The pirate with the scar slapped him on the back. As they laughed and hooted, Tom saw a dark shape snaking down from the wall towards Elenna. *A lasso!* Before he could react, it had looped over her body and pulled tight, forcing her arms to her side.

"Looks like we've got ourselves

another recruit, lads," laughed the
scarred pirate, yanking on the lasso
and dragging Elenna towards the wall.

She writhed and kicked. "Get this
off me!" she yelled.

With a cry, Tom flung his sword

towards the lasso. It spun through the air, blade flashing, and sliced the cords of rope.

Elenna landed lightly on her feet.

"You won't get away next time," snarled the pirate.

Tom picked up his sword and cut through the rope around Elenna.

"Thanks," she said. "Now, how are we going to get past them to rescue Aaron? They've got numbers and a vantage point on their side."

An idea started to form in Tom's mind. "The pirates are trying to capture people, but perhaps we need to play them at their own game. Every village has a prison, doesn't it?" he asked.

Elenna nodded.

"Remember when we first met Tagus, and we were locked up? Maybe we can find a way to get the pirates locked up, too. Then we can save Aaron – and get some of Sanpao's men out of the way. It'll make the rest of our Quest easier."

Elenna's eyes gleamed. "I like it! Prison's the least they deserve."

"We'll come back tonight," Tom said. They mounted Storm and Blizzard and started to ride away from the village wall.

"Gone so soon, you lily-livered cowards?" one of the pirates yelled after them. A bottle whistled past them, shattering on the ground.

Not for long, Tom thought, grimly. *Just you wait.*

1

LOOTING THE PIRATES

Tom and Elenna set up camp behind a boulder, out of view of the village. The ash-gritty ground was covered in footprints, which Tom guessed had been made by the fleeing villagers.

Elenna and Tom settled down to a simple supper. Fountains of lava were shooting up from the volcano, casting a burning light across the sky.

The Tree of Being is out there somewhere, Tom thought uneasily. *I just hope Sanpao hasn't found it yet.*

"So how are we going to get the pirates into prison?" Elenna asked between mouthfuls.

Tom took a gulp of water from his flask. "With the amount of food and drink they've stolen, they'll be guzzling away. They'll soon be fast asleep. Let's take their weapons and use them to lure the pirates to prison," Tom replied.

Elenna's bright eyes gleamed with amusement. "So we'll be looting from the looters!"

Tom jumped to his feet. "It's dark enough now," he said. "Come on – the sooner we do this, the sooner we can get on with our Quest. And Sanpao will have fewer men to stop us."

Elenna kicked dirt over the fire to extinguish it. Tom swung his shield over his shoulder, put one foot into Storm's stirrup, and grabbed the reins to pull himself up.

They cantered towards the village walls. Tom squinted in the darkness. The walls were empty of pirates now.

Tom and Elenna halted the horses and listened for a few moments. It was silent, save for the dull rumble of the volcano.

"The pirates must be sleeping off everything they've eaten and drunk," whispered Tom.

He guided Storm so that the stallion was standing right against the wall.

Tom stood up in the saddle and reached for the wall's top, gripping a ridge in the stonework. He bent his knees then sprang up, hooking his left leg over the wall. He scrambled across it and leaped down, landing on a platform.

A flight of stone steps led down into the streets. Torches hung among the scorched and damaged buildings. Their faint glow was enough for Tom to make out heaps of rubble and an open space in the centre, which he guessed was the village square.

He looked back over the wall to see Elenna already standing on Storm's saddle. He leaned down towards her, his hand outstretched. She grabbed it, and used her feet to scale the wall while Tom pulled her up and over.

They crept down the steps and into the village streets. Elenna tugged at Tom's sleeve and pointed at a thick wall and wooden door set underneath the flight of stairs. There were bars in the tiny window at the top of the door.

"The prison," she whispered.

The door was ajar, the key dangling in the lock. On either side of the frame was a wooden slot, into which a plank could be fitted to make the door secure. Tom pushed it open, wincing as the hinges creaked. He grinned. "Perfect – it's empty."

They turned back towards the village square, cautiously passing ruined houses, and lanes that were littered with upturned or half-empty barrels of food.

Tom could hear a rasping noise coming from the direction of the village square. "Sounds like snoring," he murmured.

He and Elenna made their way towards the square. They ducked behind a broken cart and peered out. The market stalls had hammocks strung between them, and in each slept a snoring pirate. Some mumbled in their sleep, while others scratched and twitched.

One gave a belch and rubbed his belly. "Cursed Avantian grub," he muttered in his sleep.

Tom silently beckoned Elenna forward. They crept out from behind

the cart and in among the pirates. In
a far corner of the square, Tom saw a
small figure huddled on the ground
– Aaron. His cheeks shone damply in
the torchlight, and Tom guessed that
he'd cried himself to sleep.

Some of Sanpao's crew had
their weapons with them in their

hammocks, but most had thrown them carelessly to the ground. Tom could see that Elenna already had a crossbow and a cutlass. He ducked to pick up a dagger from underneath a hammock, careful not to disturb the pirate above, drool trickling from his open mouth as he slept.

Tom shoved the dagger into his hide belt and picked up a cat-o'-nine-tails that was leaning against a post. The pirate in the next hammock let out great, grunting snores. His mouth gaped and Tom caught the glint of a gold tooth in the moonlight.

Our friend from earlier, he thought. *And what have we here?*

Nestled by one of the pirate's thick

arms was a cutlass with a golden hilt and scabbard.

Slowly, Tom took hold of it, gently teasing the weapon out of the hammock. He grinned when it came clear, turning the cutlass in his hand. Its gleaming blade was engraved with intricate patterns, its beautiful

hilt studded richly with jewels.

Who did you steal this from? Tom wondered.

But as he stepped away, his foot nudged one of the many empty bottles on the ground. It rolled into the metal frame of a market stall with a clank.

The gold-toothed pirate jerked bolt upright. "What scurvy dog goes there?" he snarled.

1

THE TRAP IS SET

Tom dropped to the ground and rolled under the hammock. He lay still, his heart hammering as the pirate shifted around. Across the square he could see that Elenna had crouched low at the foot of one of the posts. There was a swishing sound as the pirate drew his dagger; above him, Tom could see his outstretched arm, jabbing the air with his blade.

"Cursed land's got me imagining things," muttered the pirate. The hammock swung as he lay back down again. "Sooner we find that Tree, the better." With a snort, the rise and fall of his snores soon started again.

Tom exhaled a long sigh of relief. He saw Elenna get to her feet and he rolled out soundlessly, the cutlass still in his hand.

He moved quickly around the other hammocks, gathering the remaining weapons, then knelt beside Aaron. He shook the boy's shoulder gently.

Aaron's eyes flew open. Tom clamped a hand over his mouth before he could cry out.

"It's all right," Tom whispered. "We're here to rescue you. Follow me."

Aaron nodded, and they hurried through the square, ducking behind the broken cart. Elenna squatted down beside them, her arms full of blades and arrows. One of Tom's cutlasses clanked against a crossbow, the sound like a bell ringing across the dark square. They stiffened, but the pirates carried on snoring.

"We're going to get the pirates out of the way now," Tom explained to Aaron. "Stay out of sight – and use this if you have to." He gave him a dagger, then turned to Elenna. "Come on, let's get our loot to the prison."

They crept out of the square and back through the ruined streets. Once they reached the cell under the stone steps, Tom opened the creaking door and they piled the weapons at the back. The torches outside made them gleam.

"It looks just like a pile of treasure," Tom said. "The pirates are sure to take a look. I'll go and wake them up, then run on ahead and hide there." He pointed to a space behind the door, in the cell. "You can wait

on the steps above us with this."
Tom passed Elenna one of the looted
blades, a long rapier that would fit
across the slots on either side of the
door. "Once the pirates are inside, I'll
run out, and you jump down to help
me lock the door."

Elenna tilted her head. "Sounds
good – except for one thing." She
pressed the rapier back into Tom's
hand. "I should be the one who
wakes the pirates and hides in here."

"But that means you'll be in the
most danger, and—"

"Look at the space behind the
door," Elenna interrupted. "It's tiny.
I'm smaller than you, so I should be
the one who hides there."

Tom grinned and nodded. Not for

the first time, he felt lucky to have Elenna with him on his Quests.

He watched her set off back to the square, and when she was out of sight he climbed up the steps. Fresh flakes of ash had already covered the footprints he and Elenna had left earlier. Tom leaned over the edge of the steps, checking he was directly above the cell door. Then he crouched down, the rapier by his side.

"Ahoy there, you lily-livered lot!" Elenna's voice split the night air. Then, seconds later, she came back into view, sprinting towards the cell.

To Tom's amazement, she paused and yelled in a voice lower than her usual tone, "There be a crock of booty awaiting us!"

Tom had to stifle a laugh. His friend was pretending to be a pirate!

The pirates staggered up the street after Elenna, yawning and stretching. But their pace quickened when Elenna shouted, "It's in this here cell," and darted inside.

"Look at that, lads!" shouted the pirate with the scar on his face. "Gold! We're going to be the richest crew that ever sailed the skies."

The torchlight lit up their grins and shining eyes as they shoved and jostled their way in after Elenna.

Tom hoped she'd had time to hide. He drew himself up, ready to spring.

"That's not booty," Tom heard another of the pirates yell. "They're our weapons!"

As if this had been a signal, Elenna shot out of the prison. Tom sprang from the steps to the ground beside her, the rapier in his hand. They both slammed the door shut.

"What's going on?" one of the trapped pirates yelled.

"Quick," gasped Tom, as the pirates started shoving against the door.

He and Elenna slid the rapier into the wooden slots on each side of the door frame, holding it fast. Tom turned the key in the lock and tucked it into his jerkin. The pirates kicked and punched from the other side, but the door didn't budge.

One of the pirates looked out of the window by the window. "You wait until we get out of here," he hissed.

"We'll dip you in a pot of boiling tar and toss you off our ship. You'll be sorry you were born!"

"You'll be the sorry ones, matey," retorted Elenna in her pirate voice.

The two of them ran back to the square. "Sanpao's a few men down now," Tom gasped, as they dashed along the street. "And they won't be snatching any more children for their crew."

"Aaron!" Elenna called as they reached the square. "You're safe!"

The boy peered out from behind the cart. Then he broke into a grin of delight and rushed towards them.

"You do a good pirate's voice!" he told Elenna with a wide smile.

Elenna gave him a hug and tousled

his hair. "Let's get you out of here."

They raced back to the stone steps to the wall and scrambled over it. Tom whistled to Storm and Blizzard and they trotted over.

"What were you doing all the way over there?" wondered Elenna, smoothing Blizzard's mane.

"Hiding," said Tom grimly, crouching to look at bootprints in the ash. The soles each had the outline of the Beast's skull. "More pirates must have passed this way. Lots of them." Tom stood and followed the trail with his eyes. His chest tightened. "They're heading towards the Vanished Woodland – and the Tree of Being. There's no time to waste."

Elenna glanced towards Aaron,

who was stroking Storm's muzzle. "We can't bring him with us," she said quietly. "It's too dangerous."

A figure stepped out from behind a mound of rocks. Tom's hand curled around his sword as a flash of fire from the volcano lit the sky. It was Aaron's mother, her baby clutched to her hip. With a cry, she ran towards Aaron and embraced him.

"Thank you!" she said to Tom and Elenna. "How can I ever repay you?"

"By safely reaching the City," Tom replied, looking at her.

He and Elenna watched the woman and her children disappear.

"That's one person freed from the pirates," Tom said. "Now we need to save the rest of the kingdom."

THE VANISHED WOODLAND

"Tom... Tom!" Elenna was calling.

Tom opened his eyes. The early morning light was made as dingy as ditchwater by the ash suspended in the sky.

They'd travelled through most of the night and were now much closer to the volcano. Fountains of burning lava still erupted from its crater.

"We must be near the Vanished Woodland," said Elenna. She pointed at the footprints that snaked across the ground ahead, bearing the tell-tale skull pattern. "And look, these tracks come from another direction. Sanpao must have looting parties all over Avantia."

Tom noticed a grey-green shadow at the foot of the mountain. It was a band of trees, their branches quivering. The light shifted, and the shadow faded, but then reappeared – as soft as a ribbon of silk. It was a forest, taking form and then vanishing again.

"There it is!" Tom cried. "The Vanished Woodland."

"I can guess how it got its name,"

said Elenna, with a broad grin.

It wasn't until they reached the outskirts of the woodland that it seemed to stay solid. The ash was denser the closer they came to the volcano, and Tom saw that both the pirates' prints and those left by the horses were as deep as the length of his thumb. Elenna's eyes were red and watery, and Tom's mouth and nose felt full of the bitter-tasting flakes. Every leaf and branch of the woodland was veiled with ash.

Somewhere in there is the Tree of Being, Tom thought. *But where?*

They left Storm and Blizzard on the edge of the forest, somewhere sheltered from the ash so they could breathe. "Stay here and rest, boy," said

Tom, patting Storm's long, black neck. Storm whinnied and nuzzled Tom's hair while Elenna patted Blizzard farewell.

Tom and Elenna stepped among the trees. The wisps of ash trailing from their leaves and falling in grey showers made the trees look like rows of spectres.

The pirates' footprints led deep into the wood. Tom and Elenna followed them, checking around for signs of movement.

"If the pirates are here, the next Beast won't be far away," said Tom. He drew his sword, while Elenna fitted an arrow to her bow.

They were approaching a glade. Tom gasped. In the centre of the clearing, through the rows of grey-white trunks, he could see one that was still brown. It towered high above the other trees, its trunk as broad as Tom's arm span. The bark gleamed like polished leather. Clusters of dark green buds uncurled into leaves, sparkling like ornate shards of emerald and jade.

"The Tree of Being," Tom breathed.

They went up to its trunk, running their hands over its smooth surface.

"I can hardly believe it was a withered, spindly thing when we first saw it," said Elenna.

"It's becoming stronger with each Quest we complete," Tom replied. "If we drive Sanpao from the kingdom, maybe its full strength will return."

And I will have my mother back, he thought. He pictured her strong, noble face. Did she know that Tom was thinking of her – and trying to save her?

While they had been standing by the Tree, dense swirls of ash had closed around them. Tom could only just make out the other trees in the woodland. His skin prickled all over. An instinct honed over many Quests told him that something evil lurked nearby, hidden in the ash.

Whoosh! A net flashed down by his left shoulder. It snared onto the tokens on his shield and whipped back, dragging it from his arm and up, into the surrounding trees.

HECTON ATTACKS

Tom held out his sword, whirling round as he stared up into the thick ash. It was making his eyes stream, but even when he wiped them with his sleeve he still couldn't see where his shield had gone. Elenna trained an arrow upwards, but she aimed it uncertainly from side to side.

Tom sheathed his blade and peered upwards. The clouds seemed less heavy around the woodland canopy. Tom seized hold of the trunk of a tree, making its ash coat shower away. It was sturdy, but narrow enough for him to grip its sides with his arms and legs.

"I'm going up," he said. "No one steals my shield!"

He shimmied up the trunk. Elenna scaled the tree beside him, nimbly seizing a low branch and hoisting herself onto it.

As Tom climbed, the ash thinned, and he could see through the Vanished Woodland.

"Tom!" Elenna called in surprise.

He followed the line of her pointing finger and saw a hut built around the top of a tree trunk.

Its walls were woven from thin
branches, and the leaf-covering of
the roof was just visible underneath
its dusting of ash. Its door gaped
open, showing a drift of dust
gathered inside. In the distance, Tom

could make out more huts, clustered throughout the canopy, their doors open, too.

"Those huts look like they've been recently abandoned," Tom said.

"Maybe they left to escape the ash," suggested Elenna. "Or..."

They stared at each other.

"Or to escape Sanpao's Beast," Tom finished for her.

Elenna swung herself over to another tree, hoping to see more. They two friends climbed higher.

As he heaved himself through the branches, Tom peered across the canopy. "It's no good," he called over to Elenna. "I still can't see anything."

But Elenna was staring at the ground beneath them, her face pale.

Tom looked down. A ripple of green mist was curling through the ash cloud. It looked like a blemish of mould, twisting and coiling towards them. As it drifted around Tom's feet he suddenly clamped his hand over his mouth and nose. His stomach writhed. The green mist gave off a stench like rotting flesh.

The mist seemed to slice the ash cloud away, then vanished to reveal a tall figure. At first Tom thought it was a huntsman. But, as the plumes of ash cleared, he saw that the figure's flesh was a putrid green, and hanging from its belt was a net – and Tom's shield. The creature's mouth was wide open, and the green mist was billowing out of it.

Tom glanced at Elenna, who held her sleeve over her mouth and nose. She nodded, and he knew she was thinking the same as him: *Sanpao's Evil Beast.*

A breeze shivered through the woodland, flapping the Beast's cape. It was sewn from the bodies of dozens of creatures. Tom could see tails and ears and feathers, all meshed together in a tapestry of death. At the top of the cape, hollowed out to form a hood, was a horned bull's head. Flies buzzed over the cape's decaying surface, and blood and pus dripped down it.

With a snarl that made the branches shudder, the Beast leapt into the air, his cape flying out

behind him. He landed on the trunk
of Tom's tree, slamming into it with
a force that made the branches
shake and quiver. His mouth twisted
into a grin and he began climbing

towards Tom, gripping the bark with his clawed hands, his movements as smooth as a spider's.

"Hecton comes for you," the Beast growled. "I will snatch your body, and you will join the other creatures."

Tom tried to climb away from Hecton, but towards the top of the tree, the spindly topmost branches snapped. He could see Elenna scrambling out along a branch of her tree, trying to reach him. It dipped under her weight, forcing her back towards the trunk.

"There's no escape," mocked Hecton. Puffs of mist escaped his mouth when he spoke.

Tom heard pitiful groans and cries, and realised they were coming from the creatures in the cape. Their glassy eyes rolled and he saw that the stitching which passed through their bodies was stretched taut.

The Beast had almost reached him: the horns on the bull's head would soon be close enough to stab his feet. Tom looked around wildly. Elenna's face in the next tree was white with horror. He couldn't go up, and the other trees were too far away to jump to.

He was trapped.

This may be the last Beast I face, Tom thought, *but I'll fight to the end.*

A VOICE ON THE AIR

Gripping the tree with one hand, Tom drew his sword with the other, pointing it down towards Hecton. "Stay back!" he shouted.

The Beast laughed, a gurgling sound like a creature being sucked into a marsh. He reached into his cape and brought out a trident, its three prongs glittering. With a low growl, he swung his arm back over his shoulder.

"Tom, look out!" yelled Elenna from her tree.

Hecton flung his trident at Tom.

Tom twisted aside and it thudded into the spot where he'd been. But its points, which were embedded in the bark, had snared the edge of his jerkin.

Tom seized the handle of the trident, trying to prise it free, but it wouldn't budge.
Not only was

he trapped at the top of the tree, but now he was pinned against the trunk.

Panic fluttered inside him as Hecton clambered ever closer. The stench of the Beast's rotting cloak was making him feel sick. He turned his sword upside-down, so he could slice through his jerkin with its blade, but Tom's head was swimming, and he fumbled his grip.

His sword spun through the ash cloud to the ground.

Trapped. And unarmed...

Tom had never felt more helpless. Hecton was grinning up at him, his dark eyes boring into him. Tom could feel sweat trickling down his face as a surge of nausea rose in his throat. He closed his eyes, shivering.

"No, Tom!" Elenna shouted.

Tom gulped down the sickness, forcing his eyes open to see an arrow whizz towards the tree. It flew past Hecton's face, scratching his skin.

Elenna! She was crouched on a sturdy branch, her bow raised.

Hecton's clawed hand reached up towards him and Tom kicked it away. The Beast slipped a little down the tree and Elenna loosed another arrow. Hecton snarled as he swiped it aside.

"Catch, Tom!" Elenna shouted.

She shot another arrow. Tom followed its flight, his eyes narrowed intently.

If I miss, it's all over, he thought.

As the arrow hurtled towards him,

Tom lunged out as far as the trident would let him and snatched at it. The plummeting shaft slid through his fingers with burning speed, but he closed his fist around the feathers at the arrow's base.

"Good work!" he called to Elenna.

He held on to one of the branches, gritting his teeth as he used the point of the arrow to slice through his jerkin. The fabric gave way and he tossed the arrow to the ground so that he could hold on to the tree with both hands.

"Look out, Tom!" Elenna yelled. "The mist!"

Hecton had let out a roar, his green features contorted. Mist wafted from his jaws with a hissing sound. It curled around Tom's ankles like the tendrils of a creeping plant.

Through the green haze, Tom saw Hecton lower his hood. His scalp writhed with the squelching bodies of hundreds of worms. They surged down the Beast's arms, dragging themselves onto the trunk and wriggling up towards Tom. They were greyish-white, their circular jaws edged with tiny, jagged teeth.

Like maggots, Tom thought. Hecton breathed another gust of green mist, which flowed around Tom's chest and face. His eyes slid shut as it filled his lungs. He was suddenly so tired. Elenna's voice rang out, high and panicked, but he didn't reply. Hecton wouldn't want him to. *And I want to*

please Hecton... he thought sleepily.

"Tom!" It was a man's voice, distant and faint. "Tom, you must fight the Beast's evil."

Tom's eyes flew open. He would know that voice anywhere. "Aduro!"

"I am by your side once more," came the Good Wizard's voice. "I am fighting Sanpao's spell – and now you must fight his body-snatcher..."

"Aduro, where are you?" Tom cried, twisting about as he searched for some sign of the Good Wizard.

A stab of pain dragged him back to the battle: the first of the worms had reached him. Its jaws fixed on the back of his hand, biting and sucking the skin. He punched it away with his other hand.

Hecton growled angrily and the creatures in his cape moaned, their eyes gummy from the green mist.

Body-snatcher! Suddenly Tom understood. Those animals had already had their bodies snatched. If he didn't get away, his own rotting carcass would be stitched into the cape, too – where he would remain for ever.

8

SANPAO'S THREAT

I can't go up, and I can't jump sideways, Tom thought. He looked down at the ground. *There's only one way out of this...*

He let go of the trunk.

As he hurtled towards Hecton, Tom stretched out and gripped the top of his shield, yanking it from the Beast's belt.

The force of his fall tore Hecton

from the tree, too. Tom heard the Beast's snarl of anger as they tumbled over and over together. Hecton's rotten cape flapped over Tom's face, making him gag, and the Beast gripped his arm. With a shout, Tom drew up his legs and thumped them into Hecton's back. The Beast gave a howl of pain, releasing Tom's arm, and spinning away into a cloud of ash.

Tom knew he only had moments before he would slam into the ground. He twisted in mid-air, fixing the shield to his arm, and called on the power of Arcta's eagle feather.

He plunged through the ash cloud and landed on his side in a mulch of damp leaves. He rolled over and got

to his feet, unhurt; the feather had done its job.

"Tom!" he heard Elenna call. She appeared through the ash cloud, sliding down the trunk of her tree to the ground. "Where's Hecton?"

Tom whirled around, but there was no sign of the Beast.

Boooom... An explosive rumble sounded in the distance, casting a flash of blue light through the ash.

"That wasn't the volcano," Elenna said, gripping her bow.

Tom shook his head grimly. "It's coming from the village."

Elenna's eyes widened. "The pirates...?"

"That's right, little girl!" crowed a voice from high up in the woodland's canopy. "I heard about your stunt in the village, and my crew are blasting their way free. Gunpowder isn't just for cannons."

Tom grabbed his sword from where it had fallen at the foot of the Tree. He and Elenna peered into the trees, Elenna pointing an arrow upwards.

"Come on, Sanpao!" Tom yelled. "Show yourself!"

The pirate king let out a mocking laugh. "What, and spoil Hecton's fun? How do you like his cape, by the way? He wants a new tunic now. Just picture it – he could make sleeves out of your arms and legs, and use your heads for pockets."

A curl of green mist reached down towards them like a rotting finger. It wrapped around Elenna's neck and head, and to Tom's horror his friend's eyes drooped.

"Sleepy," she mumbled, staggering to one side.

Tom grabbed her shoulders and shook her. "Elenna, no!" He remembered Aduro's words. "You have to fight it."

There were flecks of white in the

mist, and Tom realised that the deadly worms were dropping down around them. One had clambered onto Elenna's leg. It arched its spine and sank its jaws into the muscle behind her calf. It twisted, burrowing inside her skin. Elenna gave a gasp of pain.

Tom lunged down and prised it away with the flat of his blade. He swept his shield through the green mist, scattering it into hundreds of tiny puffs.

Somewhere in the mist around them, he heard Hecton snarl.

Elenna's eyes fluttered open. "Thanks," she said groggily. "Now let's finish this."

"My pleasure!" Sanpao yelled.

The ash-smothered woodland came to life. Pirates whipped through the trees towards Tom and Elenna, swinging on long vines. They whooped and cheered, singing snatches of song: "The scourge of land, of sky and sea, grim pirates of Makai are we!"

The men released their hold on the vines and dropped to the ground, kicking up clouds of ash.

Another figure swung down towards them, larger than the others, roaring a battle cry that echoed through the Vanished Woodland – Sanpao. He flipped through the air, landing in a crouch beside the Tree of Being. He held an enormous axe in his hand, its blade edged with what looked like long shark's teeth.

"Ahoy, my young friends." Sanpao sneered at Tom and Elenna. He drew himself up to his full height. "I'm glad you're here to see my victory."

His tattooed arms and plaited coil of hair shone greasily, and the jewels in Tom's belt glittered. The pirate king raised his axe above his head. His shoulder muscles rippled as he swung it at the Tree of Being.

"No!" yelled Tom. He hurled his sword at Sanpao. The hilt clattered against the pirate king's fist, making the axe fall from his grasp.

It missed the Tree, slicing harmlessly into the ground.

Sanpao's oily plait swung like a whip as he twisted quickly to face

Tom. "You dirty dog," he snarled. He pulled out a dagger. "By the time I've finished, Hecton won't be able to make a handkerchief from what's left of your sorry, snivelling body."

He charged at Tom, the dagger aimed at his chest.

Tom leapt up and out of his way by grasping the lowest branch of the Tree of Being. He swung his legs, wrapping them around the branch, and pulled himself onto it. He held his arms outstretched, balancing on the smooth, brown surface.

Sanpao skidded to a halt and turned back, his face red with rage.

"And by the time we're finished, Sanpao," Tom said, "you'll wish you'd never heard of Avantia!"

9

BATTLE AMONG THE TREES

Tom could suddenly sense the air throbbing around him, and the branch beneath his feet vibrated and hummed. Something was happening.

The Tree's giving me strength, he realised. *It wants me to defeat the pirate king.*

Sanpao was snarling up at him. His crew circled around the Tree, then one of them charged at Elenna with his cutlass. Stepping nimbly aside, she slashed an arrow at him like a dagger; the tip grazed his thick neck, making him drop his weapon. His cry of surprise made Sanpao glance towards him.

Tom leapt from the branch, landing on Sanpao's shoulders. The pirate king crumpled, striking his head on an exposed tree root. Tom jumped clear as his enemy leaped to his feet. Sanpao's eyes were dark with hatred. He rushed at Tom, his dagger thrust out towards him. Tom jumped and caught hold of the branch again, drawing up his knees and thumping his feet into Sanpao's chest. The pirate king staggered backwards, his

breath coming in harsh rasps.

Elenna shot at a pirate attempting
to fix an arrow to a crossbow,
splintering its wooden frame. Then
other pirates emerged through
the Vanished Woodland, and Tom
guessed they were the men he and
Elenna had imprisoned.

One of them shoved the pirate with
the crossbow aside. "I'll be dealing

with this scurvy scum," he said, and Tom recognised the glitter of his gold tooth when he spoke.

In the pirate's hand was a spiked ball and chain. He advanced on Elenna, whirling it above his head as another of Sanpao's crew charged her from the side, aiming a cat-o'-nine-tails. She needed help – and quickly...

Tom reached for his sword, but it wasn't hanging by his hip. *Oh, no,* he thought, remembering that it was still lying where he had thrown it at Sanpao's axe. But there was something else tucked into his hide belt: Koron's fang.

He pulled out the fang and hurled it at the gold-toothed pirate. It spun over and over on itself as it sliced through the air, then struck the pirate on the side of his neck. He dropped his ball and chain. The fang disappeared, leaving a black mark, like mildew, on the pirate's skin. His body went rigid, his mouth froze mid-shout, his eyes unblinking. He toppled to the ground and lay as stiffly as a fallen tree.

"I can't move!" he shouted. "Help!"

"Thanks, Tom," called Elenna, as the pirate grunted and growled. "Looks like we won't have to worry about him for a while."

She swivelled, training her bow on the pirate with the cat-o'-nine-tails. But he was staring at his frozen companion. With a cry of terror, he hurtled off through the trees.

"Where do you think you're off to?" Sanpao bellowed after him. "Yellow-dog coward!"

Tom ran and picked up his sword.

The pirate king had yanked his shark's tooth axe from the ground and slung it over his shoulder. They stood on either side of the Tree of Being, slowly circling the trunk.

"You don't give up, do you?" Sanpao said, his cruel mouth curled into a sneer.

Tom shook his head. "Never. I would fight to the death to rid Avantia of your evil presence."

Sanpao laughed – a long bellow of mirth that seemed to rattle in his chest like a box of bones. "Surely you can't really believe that your silly

Quests are worth dying for?" he asked.

Tom nodded. "I'm fighting for my kingdom – and my mother. I would gladly give my life for either."

"Well, I'll help you prove it some time," said Sanpao. "But not now."

The pirate king clicked his fingers. The swirling clouds of ash lifted, cleaved apart by the pirates' floating ship. Its wooden hull creaked as it floated down towards them. Its masts were hung with red and black sails, each marked with the Beast skull symbol. The largest mast was a branch Sanpao had already stolen from the Tree of Being. Cannons were visible through the hatches in the ship's sides, and it was encrusted all over with rotting black barnacles.

The pirates already on board
tossed ropes over the side, which
snaked down to the ground. The crew
seized hold of them, clambering up
hand over hand and onto the ship.

Sanpao gave Tom and Elenna a
mocking salute, grabbed one of the
ropes, and hoisted himself up.

Tom watched him, leaning on
his sword. "Wait!" he called as

something occurred to him. "Did you make the volcano erupt?"

Sanpao paused and looked down. "Of course I did! Who else would want to empty the region and steal its loot? I told you my gunpowder was useful. I dropped a load of it inside the crater and – boom! I made my very own volcanic eruption!"

He scrambled up the rope, after the other pirates, and onto the ship. It rose up, until it seemed the size of a bird, and sailed out of sight.

Elenna was collecting her arrows, wiping their tips clean. "Why didn't you try to stop Sanpao?" she asked.

Tom turned to gaze over the woodland. "We've still got a Beast to face," he said.

THE CREATURES IN THE CAPE

"If we don't defeat Hecton, he'll kill every creature he can," Tom said. "We've seen how dangerous he is."

Elenna nodded. "You're right."

Tom saw the Beast moving towards them through the trees, just visible through a shroud of green mist.

"Duck!" he yelled.

Elenna flung herself to the ground

and Tom hurled his shield, sending it spinning towards the Beast.

Hecton gave a howl of pain as the shield struck his midriff, and he sank to his knees.

As Tom and Elenna charged towards him, Tom saw that the Beast had a jagged branch stuck through his upper arm. *That must have happened when he fell,* Tom realised.

The green mist coiled around Hecton, and the white worms from his head tumbled onto his arm, nibbling at his skin with their busy jaws. Hecton groaned and batted them away. He sank to his knees, the mist making his eyes roll shut.

"That's it!" Tom called to Elenna. "Our weapons can only do so much.

We have to get Hecton to turn his magic on himself – make the Beast devour his own body!"

When they reached the struggling Beast, Tom darted around him, dodging his flailing limbs. As Hecton reached upwards, Tom snatched the net from where it was hooked inside his belt. Elenna ran behind Hecton. The worms were crawling over his injured arm, and when the Beast curled up with a bellow of pain, Tom threw the net over him. Elenna pulled an arrow from her quiver, using it to pin the net to the ground. Tom stretched his side of the net taut and rammed a fallen branch through it to secure it.

The wriggling creatures crawled

over the trapped Beast. Tom saw one of them burrow inside Hecton's chest, leaving a tiny oozing tunnel. Another disappeared into his thigh.

But Hecton's eyes flashed and he began to squirm beneath the net. "None can defeat me," he snarled. "Prepare to die."

With a hiss, he punched forwards with his trident, slicing a gash through the net. It collapsed around him and he leaped free, his rotting cloak left crumpled on the ground behind him. Elenna aimed an arrow at the Beast but his movements were too quick.

Tom grabbed his shield and braced himself against the charging Beast. Hecton thrust his trident towards

Tom's chest, but Tom deflected the blow with a swipe of his sword. The ringing clash of metal echoed through the trees. Hecton grabbed the edge of his cape, making the creatures stitched into it give a high-pitched moan. The sound sent a chill down Tom's spine.

"You will become one of them," Hecton yelled. He swung the cape at Tom, trying to envelop him in its gruesome folds.

Pus flicked from the creatures' bodies, raining on Tom in thick yellow blobs. The slick surface of the cape skimmed over him and Tom gave a cry of revulsion. He held his breath against the stench and dropped to the ground, rolling free of its folds.

Hecton swung the cape at him again, but a zipping arrow from Elenna thudded into his shoulder. The Beast howled with rage and Tom leapt aside.

I've got to trap Hecton inside that cape, Tom realised, shaking the slime from his hands.

As Hecton lifted his cape and swooped at him again, Tom stepped to the left. Hecton followed, but Tom sprang to the right instead. The cape swirled through empty air, then wrapped around the Beast. He tried to struggle out, but the sticky insides of the cape seemed to stick to his skin, the rotting bodies of all those caught animals smothering him.

"No..." Hecton howled. The

creatures' cries rose to a shrill
scream of revenge, as if they were
delighting in their victory over their
master. The worms pushed into him
until none of his body remained.

Hecton's eyes fixed on Tom then

closed. The pile of worms collapsed, then, with a final hiss of green mist, melted away into the ground.

Tom exhaled a long breath. He sank to the ground, exhausted. Elenna flopped down next to him. "We did it," Tom panted.

"I can't remember a more revolting Beast," said Elenna with a shudder.

She blinked suddenly. A raindrop slid down her face, leaving a clean trail through the ash.

They grinned at each other and looked up at the sky.

Fat raindrops splattered through the Vanished Woodland, washing the grey ash from the trees and leaving vibrant shades of green in its place.

Tom got up. "Sanpao's evil is going."

The rotting cape and trident lay on the patch of ground where Hecton had disappeared. Tom picked up the trident. It was too large to slide into his belt, so he slung it over his shoulder. "Hecton's token," he said. "We'll find out what powers it has soon enough."

A flash of movement caught Tom's eye. The cape was twitching. They stared, amazed, as a rabbit wriggled its way out. It sat still for a moment, its nose snuffling, then bounded into the undergrowth. Then the snout of a fox poked through the folds. It trotted away, swishing its brush. The creatures were coming back to life!

Elenna's eyes shone. "Hecton's evil is being reversed," she breathed.

The cape fizzed with sparks of red and purple light. Tom and Elenna ducked behind a bush so as not to startle the emerging creatures. Birds fluttered out, singing as they soared away; mice scurried free, and grass snakes slithered through the bushes, their tongues flickering. There was a low bellow and a magnificent bull thrust its way out. His muscular

flanks shone and he tossed his head, his horns gleaming as he charged into the Woodland.

His skull formed the hood of the cape, Tom remembered.

Elenna clutched his arm and pointed through the leaves at the final creature to emerge. But it wasn't a creature – it was a boy.

He was dressed in a tunic made of bark, his long hair tied back with a length of creeper. He rubbed his eyes and seized hold of a vine, hoisting himself up and swinging away through the branches.

"He must be a Tree Dweller," said Tom. "One of the people who lives in those huts."

The two friends made their way

through the Vanished Woodland, back to where Storm and Blizzard would be waiting for them.

Tom glanced over his shoulder for a final look at the Tree of Being. It was already sinking into the ground, its branches curled around its thick trunk as it drilled into the earth.

Tom knew that it would soon emerge in a new location. The pirates would be waiting to capture it, but so would Tom. And the tree was getting stronger all the time – soon a portal would appear into the world where Freya and Silver were held prisoner, and Tom would have them back.

But in the meantime...

Are you ready for our next battle, Sanpao? he thought. *I know I am.*

CONGRATULATIONS, YOU HAVE COMPLETED THIS QUEST!

At the end of each chapter you were awarded a special gold coin.
The QUEST in this book was worth an amazing 11 coins.

Look at the Beast Quest totem picture inside the back cover of this book to see how far you've come in your journey to become

MASTER OF THE BEASTS.

The more books you read, the more coins you will collect!

Do you want your own
Beast Quest Totem?

1. Cut out and collect the coin below
2. Go to the Beast Quest website
3. Download and print out your totem
4. Add your coin to the totem
www.beastquest.co.uk/totem

READ THE BOOKS, COLLECT THE COINS!
EARN COINS FOR EVERY CHAPTER YOU READ!

550+ COINS
MASTER OF
THE BEASTS

410 COINS
HERO

350 COINS
WARRIOR

230 COINS
KNIGHT

180 COINS
SQUIRE

44 COINS
PAGE

8 COINS
APPRENTICE

Don't miss the next exciting Beast Quest book, TORNO THE HURRICANE DRAGON!

Read on for a sneak peek...

CHAPTER ONE

THE ROAD NORTH

Tom tugged on Storm's reins, drawing his black stallion to a halt, and pulled out the tree-bark map from his saddlebag. He and Elenna had been riding fast and had reached the very edge of Avantia's Central Plains. The Northern Mountains reared up ahead, their forbidding rocky peaks outlined against the sky.

Tom unrolled the map and peered at the outlines of Avantia's roads, rivers and hills, then shook his head. "The Tree of Being still hasn't appeared," he told Elenna.

Elenna manoeuvred closer on her white mare, Blizzard, so that she could lean over and look at the map.

"It's never taken this long before," she said. "We need something to tell us where to find it. Otherwise…"

Elenna didn't finish her thought. She didn't need to.

Tom rolled up the map and put it away, trying not to think about what would happen if Sanpao and his pirates caught up with them. He and Elenna needed to get to the Tree of Being first.

Tom pulled his golden compass out of his saddlebag. "The needle is still pointing towards Destiny," he said. "We should press on northwards."

"If the Tree of Being reappears in the south or west," Elenna murmured anxiously, "we're in big trouble. What if it's wrong?"

"The compass has never steered us wrong before," said Tom. Stowing away the compass, he urged Storm into a trot. As they moved on, Tom glanced over his shoulder to see that the last traces of the forest had disappeared behind them. He and

Elenna were tired from their battle with Hecton the Body Snatcher, but Tom knew that they couldn't rest yet. Avantia was still under the gravest threat it had ever known.

"We have to get to the Tree first," Tom muttered to himself. "If Sanpao the Pirate King gets his hands on it, he'll be able to use its powers to raid any other land he likes."

But that wasn't the only reason why Tom's stomach churned at the thought of losing the race with the pirates. The Tree of Being would also open up a portal to Tavania, where Tom's mother, Freya, and Elenna's pet wolf, Silver, had been left stranded at the end of their last Beast Quest.

Getting to the Tree first is our

only chance of rescuing them, Tom thought grimly. "Sanpao may be clever," he said, "but we can out-think him, and we've got the best reason in the world not to give up." He touched the trident that he had won in his combat against Hecton; he had cut off the shaft so that it would fit into his sash. "We have the weapons we need, too. Nothing can stop us!"

As he finished speaking, a fork of blue lightning crackled down from the sky. Storm reared, striking at the air with his hooves. Tom had to grip tightly with his knees to stop himself being thrown from the saddle. Blizzard let out a high-pitched whinny and stepped sideways, her hooves slipping on the stones. Elenna leaned forward, patting the nervous mare's neck soothingly.

Tom was still tugging hard on Storm's reins when the crack of lightning expanded into a shimmering blue globe, with the figure of Wizard Aduro inside it. His form was faint; Tom could still see the outline of the mountains through it.

"Aduro!" Tom glanced at Elenna. "Do you think Sanpao has sent him?" he asked her quietly.

"I don't know." Elenna's voice was sharp with suspicion. "But we shouldn't trust him."

Before Tom and Elenna set out, Sanpao had put the Good Wizard under an evil spell. During the last stage of their Quest, Aduro had managed to send a faint message to Tom that showed he was fighting with all his strength against the Dark Magic. Tom hoped that Aduro was sending another message now, to prove that Sanpao's hold on him was beginning to weaken.

Tom's hope died as he saw the cold sneer on Aduro's face and the malicious glimmer in his eyes.

Read
TORNO THE HURRICANE
DRAGON
to find out more!

Beast Quest

OUT NOW!

The epic adventure is brought to life on **Xbox One** and **PS4** for the first time ever!